For Ana, Naomi, and Sean who are
a wish come true; and for David, always. — S. L.

For Alan —T. S.

The Wish Ring

Retold by Suzanne Loebl
Illustrated by Thomas Sperling

Star Bright Books
New York

There was once a poor couple named Hans and Lena who owned a small farm at the edge of the forest. Although they worked hard on their farm, they had little success and often went hungry.

They had a barn without cows, a stable but no horses, and a barnyard with no chickens. Their only field was full of boulders, too heavy for Hans and Lena to move. Their farm was the poorest in the village.

Each spring, as Hans and Lena prepared the soil for new seeds, they hoped that their life would improve.

"This year will be a good year," Hans told Lena. "When the rains come, our seeds will grow into tall golden-yellow wheat. We will thresh the wheat and sell the grain to the miller. With the money from the miller, we will buy a cow. With the money we get from selling the cow's milk, we will buy a horse. With the help of the horse, we will be able to move the boulders from our field and then we can grow more wheat next year."

But as Hans and Lena worked, they both secretly worried. Every year, they made the same plans, but something always went wrong. One year the birds ate the seeds, another year it rained too much, and the next year it rained too little. Then there were the slugs and the bugs who ate whatever they could.

Hans gazed across their field. If he and Lena did not grow enough wheat this year, they would remain as poor as ever.

One morning as Hans was working alone in their field, he heard a faint cry.

"Help me, please help me," a voice called. It came from the forest that lay behind Hans's house. Hans stopped what he was doing and listened carefully. The cry came again.

"Help me. Please help me." Hans put down his rake and cautiously made his way into the forest.

In the forest Hans found an old woman lying on the ground. Her foot was caught in the gnarled roots of an old tree and—no matter how she struggled—she could not get free. "Please help me, please," she said. "I have been here for hours." Hans knelt down and, using all his strength, forced the roots apart.

"Thank you," said the old woman, as she pulled her foot free and rubbed it to ease the pain.

Hans offered to help the old woman home to her cottage, but she refused. "You are very kind." she said. "Now I will do something for you. Go to the far side of the forest. There, beside a grove of silver birches, you will find a large barren tree. Cut down that barren tree. When it falls, your luck will change."

Hans immediately ran home to tell Lena about the old woman.

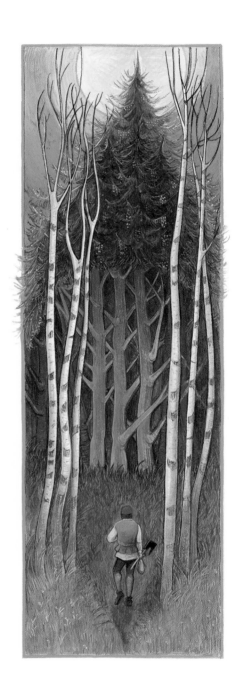

"You must hurry and leave at once," Lena said excitedly. "Perhaps the old woman has magic powers and our luck will really change. Perhaps there is some magic in that old tree."

Lena carefully wrapped some food for Hans to eat along the way, while he went to get his ax. Then Hans kissed Lena good-bye and set off.

As the old woman had instructed him, Hans walked toward the far side of the forest. He walked all day, and as the last rays of the sun sank behind the horizon, he stopped to sleep.

The next morning as sunlight broke through the trees, Hans rose and set off again.

Hans walked without resting, all the while looking eagerly for the special tree. At last he came to a barren tree that stood just beyond a grove of silver birch trees.

Hans lost no time. He raised his ax and began to chop away at the tree. He chopped and chopped until, at long last, the tree crashed to the ground with a mighty sound.

As it fell, a nest toppled from its branches. Two eggs dropped out of the nest and landed at Hans's feet.

As Hans bent to pick up the eggs, they cracked open. A young eagle stepped from one; a gold ring fell from the other.

The eagle lifted the gold ring to Hans and said, "You have set me free. This magic ring is your reward. It will grant you whatever you wish, but you have only one wish. When you know what you really want, turn the ring on your finger and say your wish out loud. But remember, you have only one wish."

The eagle grew as it spoke. When it was half as tall as Hans, it turned, spread its wings, and soared into the sky.

Hans looked at the ring. Here was luck indeed. Magic or not, a gold ring was worth more money than he or Lena had ever seen. Hans put the ring on his finger and started for home.

At dusk, Hans came to a small town. He saw a goldsmith sitting in front of his shop. "Look at my ring," he said as he held out his hand.

"It is not much to look at," the goldsmith said.

Hans laughed. "It is a magic ring," he said proudly. And he told the gold-smith all about the old woman, the barren tree, the eggs, and the eagle.

When the goldsmith heard Hans's story he said, "My friend, you must sleep at my house. It is not safe to travel at night with such a valuable ring. Besides, it will bring me good luck to have you stay here."

At dinner the goldsmith plied Hans with plenty of good food and wine. Hans was not used to eating and drinking so much, and fell asleep soon after dinner.

In the middle of the night, while Hans was dreaming of horses and cows and plenty of food, the goldsmith stealthily slipped the magic ring off Hans's finger and replaced it with one that looked exactly like it.

When the goldsmith woke Hans the next morning he said, "You must be on your way. You have a long way to go." Hans thanked the goldsmith for his kindness and they shook hands as they parted.

"You have brought me good fortune," the goldsmith said, smiling at Hans. But under his breath he added, "More than you realize."

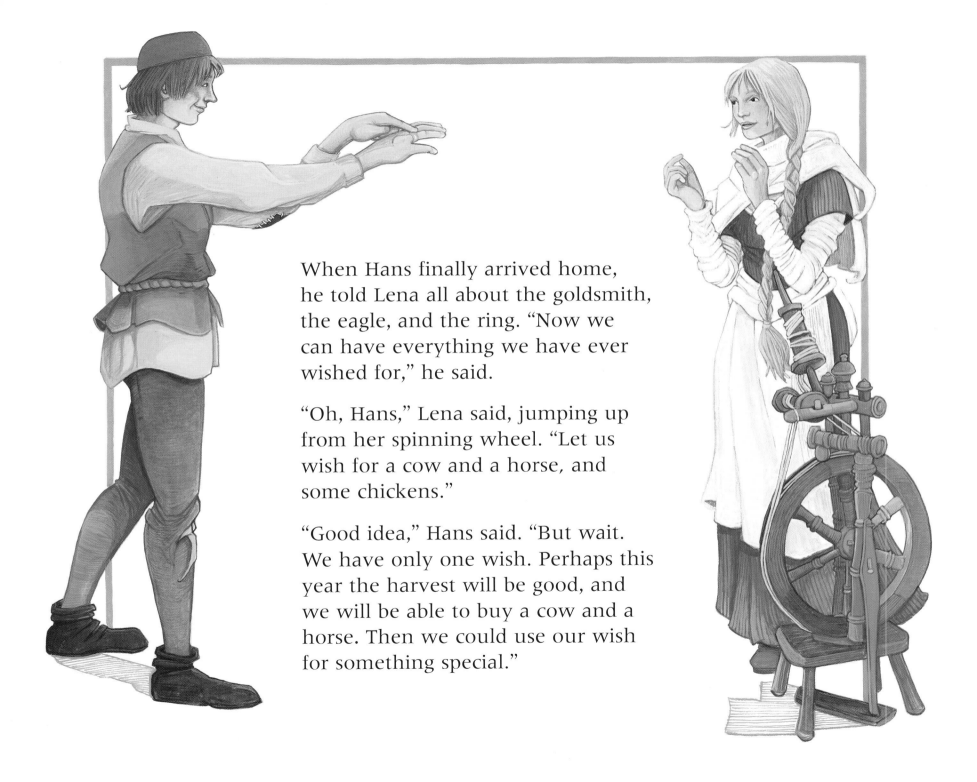

When Hans finally arrived home, he told Lena all about the goldsmith, the eagle, and the ring. "Now we can have everything we have ever wished for," he said.

"Oh, Hans," Lena said, jumping up from her spinning wheel. "Let us wish for a cow and a horse, and some chickens."

"Good idea," Hans said. "But wait. We have only one wish. Perhaps this year the harvest will be good, and we will be able to buy a cow and a horse. Then we could use our wish for something special."

That year, as they had hoped, the harvest was good. Hans and Lena had grain to sell to the miller. With the money they earned, they bought a cow and a horse. With the help of the horse, they moved the boulders from their field. And they had milk from their cow to sell.

And in the following years the harvests were good. There was grain to sell to the miller. With the money they earned, Hans and Lena bought more land, and also chickens and roosters for the barnyard. And soon there were children as well. Hans and Lena were very happy together.

One morning as they were working together in their field, Lena said, "Let us use the ring to wish for more land."

But Hans replied, "We have milk from our cow and plenty of wheat. Let us wait until after the harvest."

One evening, sometime later, when their work was done, Lena said, "Hans, why do we not use our wish? We can wish for whatever we want. We could be wealthy landowners. You could be an emperor. Our trunks could be overflowing with gold. Let us make a wish tonight."

"But we have everything we need," Hans replied. "Our life is good. We have enough land, a cow, a horse, and a wonderful family. We are still young, and life is long. "Remember, the ring has only one wish—when it is gone, it is gone for good. Be patient, and one day we will have our special wish."

Hans and Lena's good life continued. Their house was filled with laughter. There were horses in the stable, cows in the barn, chickens and roosters in the barnyard, and lots of food.

Sometimes, when Hans and Lena sat by the fire at night they would talk about how to use their wish. But one of them always said, "Wait. After the harvest we will think of something to wish for. One day we will use our wish for something very special. We have plenty of time."

As they grew older, Hans and Lena talked less and less about the wish ring. Hans often gazed at his ring and turned it on his finger, but he was always careful never to say a wish out loud. He was sure that one day he and Lena would think of something special they wanted.

Their farm kept them very busy, and as the years passed they thought of fewer and fewer things to wish for.

Hans and Lena lived until they were very old and they never ever used their wish. They never discovered that the ring was not really magic. But it did not matter. They had a very happy life and all the good fortune they could ever have wished for.

And what happened to the wicked goldsmith? No one really knows. But he did not prosper, because stolen magic always brings bad luck.